AF595853

THE VERY SUPER BEAR

NICK BLAND

A Scholastic Press book from Scholastic Australia

For Elliott – super kid.

Scholastic Press
An imprint of Scholastic Australia Pty Limited
(ABN 11 000 614 577)
PO Box 579 Gosford NSW 2250
www.scholastic.com.au

Part of the Scholastic Group
Sydney • Auckland • New York • Toronto • London • Mexico City
New Delhi • Hong Kong • Buenos Aires • Puerto Rico

First published by Scholastic Australia in 2019.
This edition published in 2020.
Text and illustrations copyright © Nick Bland, 2019.
Nick Bland asserts his moral rights as the author and illustrator of this work.

All rights reserved. No part of this publication may be reproduced or transmitted in any form or by any means, electronic or mechanical, including photocopying, recording, storage in an information retrieval system, or otherwise, without the prior written permission of the publisher, unless specifically permitted under the Australian Copyright Act 1968 as amended.

NATIONAL LIBRARY OF AUSTRALIA
A catalogue record for this book is available from the National Library of Australia

ISBN: 978-1-76097-469-5

Typeset in Geist Serifa.

Nick used acrylic paint on paper to create these illustrations.

Printed in China by RR Donnelley.

Scholastic Australia's policy, in association with RR Donnelley, is to use papers that are renewable and made efficiently from wood grown in responsibly managed forests, so as to minimise its environmental footprint.

10 9 8 7 6 5 4 3 2 20 21 22 23 24 / 2

In the Jingle Jangle Jungle,
while Bear was chasing bees,
he came across the strangest thing
beneath the shady trees.

It was such a lovely colour
and just the perfect shape.
'Today's my lucky day!' said Bear.
'I've found myself . . .

. . . A CAPE.'

He swished it here

and swooshed it there

and waved it in the breeze.

Until a little voice cried out,
'Can someone help me, please?'
It was coming from the treetops,
from way up in the sky,

where Elephant was holding tight
and trying not to cry.
'Please fly up here and save me.
I can't get down,' he said.

'It's not that kind of cape,' yelled Bear.
'I'll have to climb instead.'

As Bear climbed up the towering tree, it bent and bent . . .

. . . and bent.

The further up the tree he climbed . . .

. . . the further down they went.

When Elephant was
close enough, he stepped
right off the thing,
and gave the Very Super
Bear a very super . . .

FLING!

'Super Bear!' honked Bruce the Goose.
'Can you help us, please?
A great big yellow monster is eating all the trees.

It's gobbling up the jungle, and Owl's asleep in there.
You have to stop the monster. Please help us, Super Bear.'

'It's not that kind of cape,' said Bear.

'And I can't fly like you.'

SPLASH!

'I'm not a Super Bear,' he said.
'But I'll see what I can do.

Perhaps the monster's cranky. We should cheer it up,' said Bear.
'Let's go and pick some flowers and take them over there.'

'I might not be a Super Bear,
and I don't have superpowers,

but one thing that I know for sure . . .

. . . everyone loves flowers!’

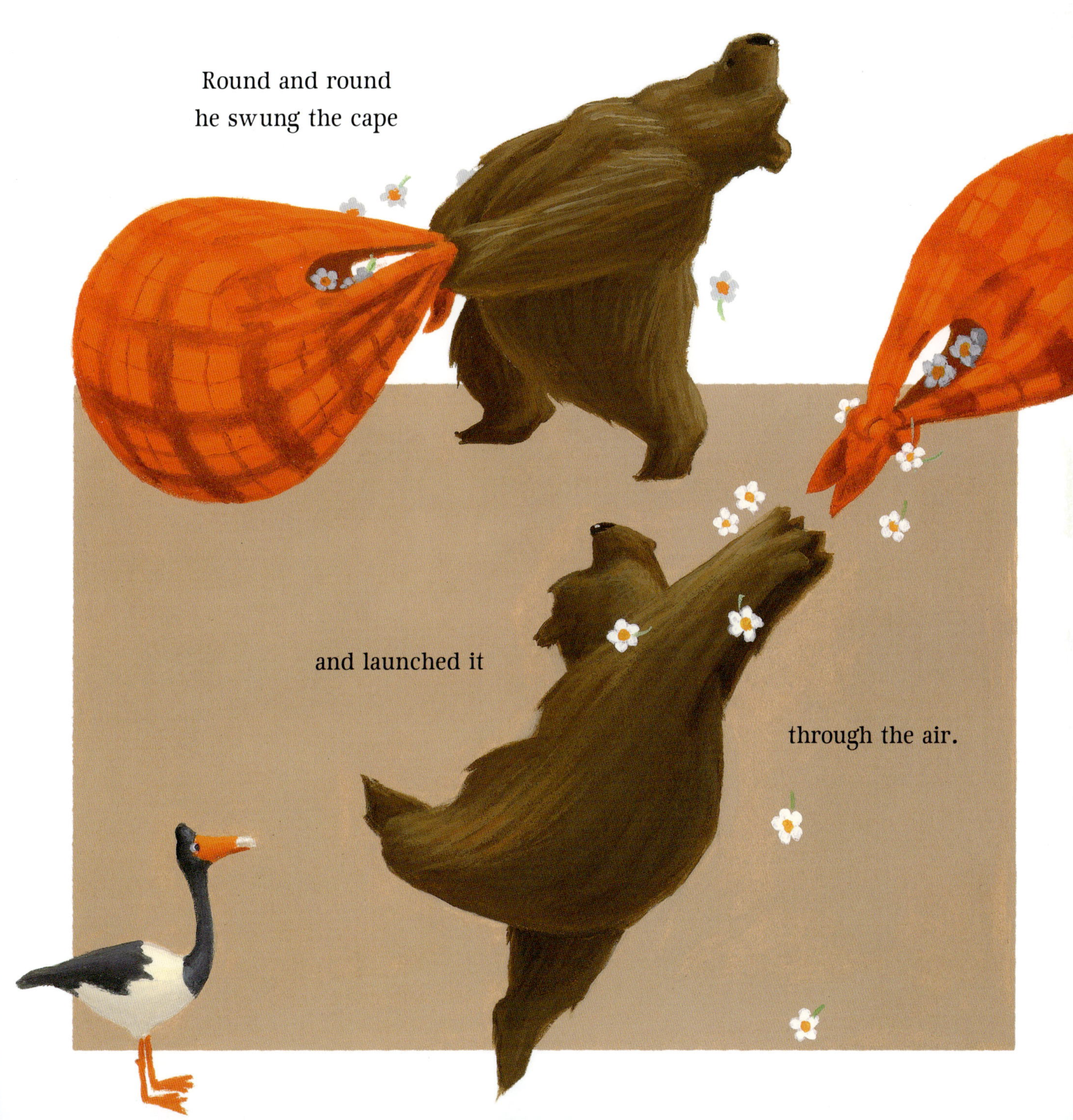

Round and round
he swung the cape

and launched it

through the air.

It landed in the monster's lap—
flowers everywhere!

The monster didn't stop at all, it kept on gobbling trees.
But wherever there are lots of flowers, there are also lots of . . .

BEES!

The monster huffed, the monster puffed, then turned and rolled away.
The Very Super Bear and Bruce had saved the jungle's day.

'A Super Bear like you,' said Owl,
'deserves a super hug.
Not only did you rescue me,
you found my picnic rug!'

They shared a moonlight picnic,
since Owl preferred the night,
and laughed about the Super Bear
and his short but super flight.